Circle

Square

Tr **Moose**

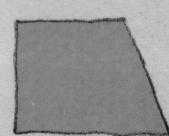

By Kelly Bingham

Pictures by Paul O. Zelinsky

ANDERSEN PRESS

For Marty, my ♡—K. B.

To my family of squares—P. O. Z.

CIRCLE, SQUARE, MOOSE
Text copyright © 2014 by Kelly Bingham.
Illustration copyright © 2014 by Paul O. Zelinsky
Originally published by Greenwillow Books,
an imprint of HarperCollins Publishers USA.
Published by arrangement with Pippin Properties, Inc.
through Rights People, London.

This paperback first published in 2014 by Andersen Press Ltd.,
20 Vauxhall Bridge Road, London SW1V 2SA.
Published in Australia by Random House Australia Pty.,
Level 3, 100 Pacific Highway, North Sydney, NSW 2060.

10 9 8 7 6 5 4 3 2 1

British Library Cataloguing in Publication Data available.
ISBN 978 1 78344 186 0

Shapes

are all around us. We see them every day. Have you ever looked at a button?

This one is a . . .

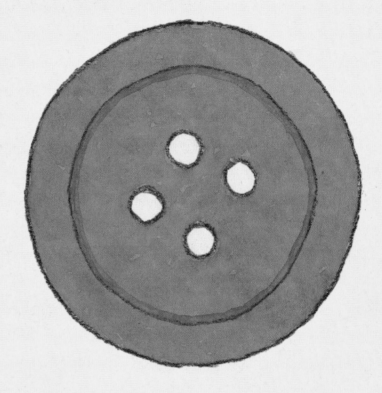

circle.

What
about
that
sandwich
you had
for lunch?

That is a . . .

square.

And if you look closely at a square, you will see that it is made of four equal sides.

Hey! Don't eat that!

Look—this is a book about shapes. Not animals. You are in the wrong book.

And please put that sandwich back. It's our square.

Now, let's learn about
triangles.
Do you know what a triangle is?

A **TRIANGLE** is . .

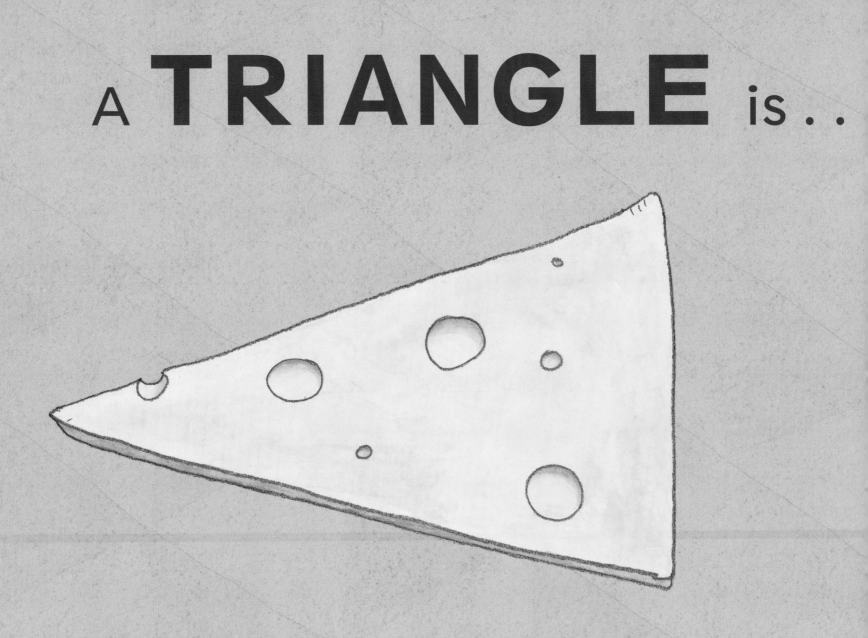

A wedge of cheese

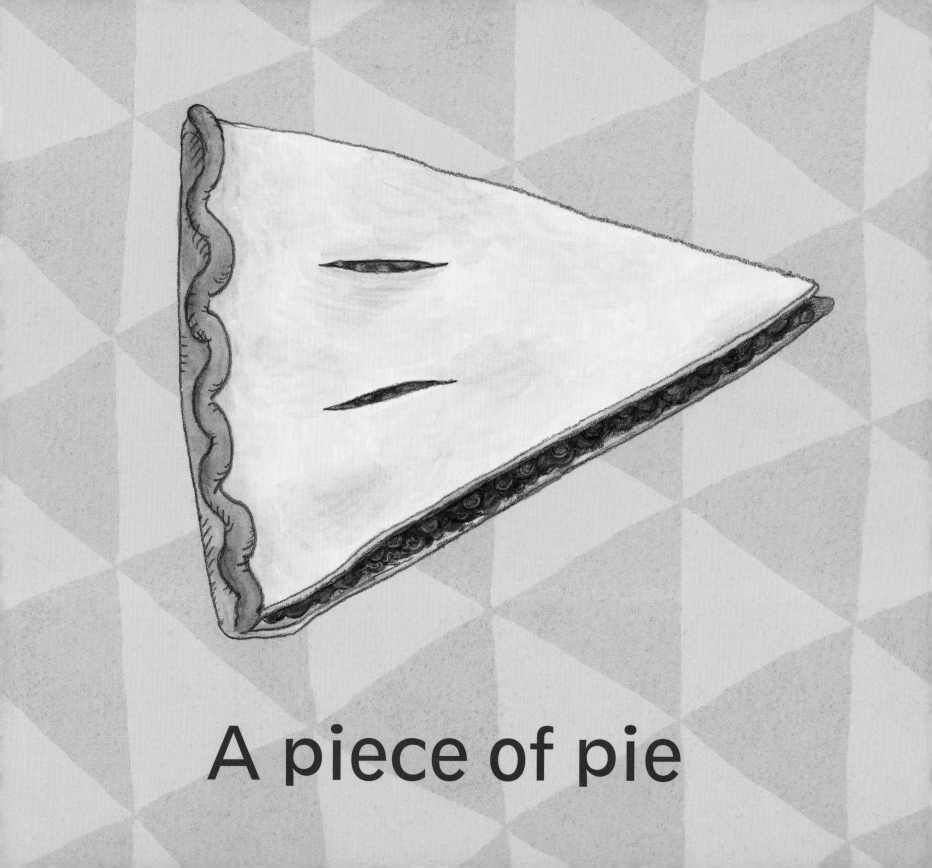

A piece of pie

Cute, but this is not an animal book. It is a shape book. You both need to leave.

Let's talk about rectangles!

A

RECTANGLE

is . . .

A domino

A book

A **DIAMOND** is . . .
The shape in a crown

A flying kite

Okay. You have to leave. You are ruining the book This is a book about shap

I'll handle this.

A **SQUARE** is . . .

A pretty picture frame

A shiny tile

Come back here!

Or a fun board game

trick

Or a ribbon's wake

A STAR

is for Zebra,
my very good friend.

Zebra and Moose.
Friends
to the
end.